PLANET 7765

THE BASIC REALITY !

BHISM NARAYAN YADAV

Made with ❤ on the Notion Press Platform
www.notionpress.com

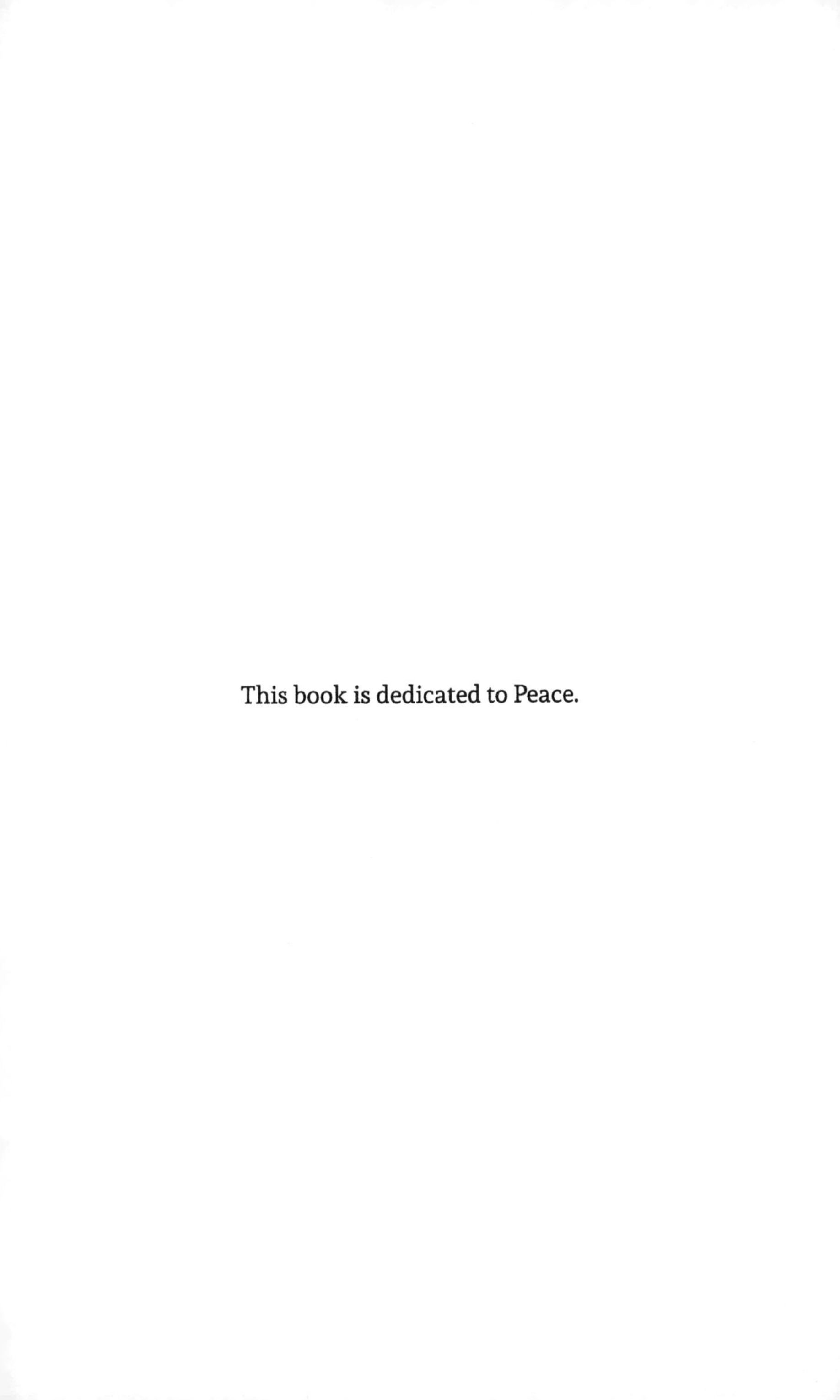

This book is dedicated to Peace.

Contents

PREFACE

Hello,

Friendships, Relationships, Money, Happiness, Caring, The Right, Ego, Responsibilities, etc. The five senses and the brain that is responsible to experience something called Life.

People share their feelings and emotions because they heard "Sharing" stories. Where to share? Whom to share? When to share? How much? And WHY? IT IS THE DATA.

Input- Eyes, Ears, Nose, Skin, Tongue

CPU- The Brain

Output- Vocal Chords, Gestures, Force

Be Wise. God Exists. The Causality Principle states that everything in this universe has a cause and an effect. You cannot make "Something" using "Nothing".

Good Luck

ACKNOWLEDGEMENTS

I want to thank my Family who is with me. My Friends who are always there for me. My Colleagues from whom I have learned

Mentors who taught me in School, College, different Institutions,

People, who corrected me when I was wrong, people who met me like a stranger to feed my brain with some amazing experiences while I was on my way.

I wish all of them very good luck.

Thank You.

PROLOGUE

Everybody wants to be happy, but what is happiness?

Nobody wants to be Sad, but what is sadness?

Everybody wants to be Rich, but what is being Rich?

Nobody wants to be poor, but what is being Poor?

This is the story of Max. Who wants to know the reality of the universe? WHY?

Because he thinks that in the age of Automobiles, Technology, Social Media content, Righteousness, and busyness are a lot of Confusion, sees the world around him and thinks Humans Change. But what change is good, and what is not?

Is there anybody who has the solution to so much Fighting for being right all the time? What is right and when to be just Quiet?

What is Influence? What are the things that influence and how to protect yourself from getting Influenced?

What is Good Influence, and what is Bad Influence?

What is Love?

I

Max

Sleep. The cheapest form of enjoyment among humans. Everybody sleeps. Sleep is important. Sometimes when you don't get good sleep you become sick. And when you sleep more than what's needed you become lazy.

Max is Poor and Lazy. Sometimes these two things are not common in the same human but he is rare. Because he has a habit of asking questions and the most important one is WHY?

He has a nice bed with a beautiful music system that plays music while he sleeps. But how can someone sleep when music banging on the eardrums? Habit is something that has made him so powerful that even the firecrackers of festivals cannot wake him up because see firecrackers burst on the outside and music playing in the closed room blocks the outside sound from entering the room.

There are different kinds of music Rock, Pop, and Metal but the best one is LO-Fi one thing because of its latest trend and second, it is made to make you sleep by changing the pitch and tempo of the track. So it feels like a new song.

There are some other types of music meditational and relaxing instrumental but the main thing is the absence of kicks and drum beats so the outside sound does not get blocked some people will feel some kind of problem while sleeping but they are also good.

The next thing is Food. There are some tremendous foods which make people get a good sleep like Kachori. Some people call them Littis but Littis and Kachoris are two brothers from different mothers because kachori has Oily Skin and Litti has Dry skin so it takes a little bit of effort of Desi Ghee to Become the cold cream of Litti.

You may be thinking the name of the chapter is Max and Here I am only talking about sleeping. Max is equal to Sleeping multiplied by laziness squared with junk food.

His mom is happy because he is as of now a college boy and does not have a lot of friends and the reason you already know. He just sleeps. Don't talk too much. Sometimes a few HMMs. and then again he just sleeps.

He is like a lizard sticked to the wall, when he sat on a couch he just be there for hours, it takes almost one hour for him to eat a meal, he sits in front of the television and eats in slow motion, listens to the same song over and over unless he gets bored and never listen to that song again, ask a lot of questions to move from one place to another as he does not find the logic and does not read the newspapers. According to him"Why should I?"

II

Love

Love is an intangible asset that has a fluctuating Goodwill sometimes negotiable too.

- Bhism Yadav

What is Love? Different kinds are there depending on person to person and situation to situation. You love your family, your friends, your career, your gadgets, your partner, your health, and your money. As I said it depends. Max is confused because the definition of love according to him is what he saw in his childhood and his childhood was filled with movies because a lazy person who loves to sleep when wakes up to fill his stomach watch television and many years back television had very limited channels but after globalization, there are a lot of television channels with different kinds of movies.

Do movies influence the emotions of a person? Yes! Everything a person Eats See, Smell, Touch, Hear, Talks, and Memorize influences the personality he is going to become.

Let us say a child is born then he loves his parents after some time he grows up he starts collecting data in his mind and get to know about different emotions.

Before he does not know the meaning of love he just knows about his Mother and Father are the two people whom he will approach in case he needs something like Food, Milk, etc. Even a small crying baby stops crying when he gets in his mother's lap. Baby is also collecting data and processing it. He is listening and learning to react to spoken words like say Dad or say mom or come here, go there, where are your eyes, where is your nose, etc.

After some time the baby grows up and starts caring for his parents. We call that love or care but for that baby, he does not know the meaning of words like love or care he just reacts.

People collect data about what to do and what not to do this is correct and this is incorrect from their environment. The definition of righteousness differs from whether the person is rich or poor, or the cities he lived or the friends he has, or the books he read. In short, a human being does something by using his brain and the brain has information that has been collected from the environment.

Nowadays the collection of data of a human being depends mostly on the movies or videos that he watches or the songs he listens to as the songs contain lyrics and lyrics contain words and words form sentences and sentences have meanings. The books he read, the stories he listened or the situations he has experienced.

Max watches movies so he gets influenced by the movies he has watched. But why do people get influenced by movies? Knowing these are just movies or recorded footage shown in a cinema theatre or Smartphones?

When I want to understand something I take the example of a child. People love to celebrate, they dance, they laugh, and when a child sees people celebrate something he thinks that this thing is good.

When he watches movies and the movie gets good business everybody talks about that movie. When he listens to some music and sees most of the people dance to that music he thinks that song is amazing. But songs contain music and lyrics. Music is sounds on a specific frequency produced by instruments arranged in a specific order. Lyrics are the words arranged on that music. Sounds release hormones, which is why people feel good when they listen to music.

Movies are recorded footage produced on a script written by a writer and directed by a director to make business and entertain or to educate or something else. To tell a story.

Human beings learn something when they see someone do something, they gather different information from different sources mix them and create something new.

In English, everything comes from the English alphabet. Humans learn the English alphabet then they learn words then sentences and to talk in that language then they gather information using that language mix them and do something new and that makes the personality of that specific human.

What is love?

Love is Care whether it is your Family, Friends, Gadgets, Health, Career, or Money. You care for "something" or "someone" and you don't want to lose that "something" or "someone" because you have developed an attachment towards that "something" or "someone". You wanted "something" because you saw some people want that "something" and you also started wanting that "something" or "some other thing" created by mixing "some things".

And when you don't get that "something" you feel bad. Because you cared for that "something" by investing time and energy and energy comes from food. People feel bad because they lost time and energy. Be wise to invest your time and energy in things that will benefit you in the future like Money. Because emotions change with information. one day you think "this" thing is good another day you get some information and "this" thing gets mixed up with "that" thing and the information updates and now your emotions and perspective will change from "this" thing towards "that" thing because you learned some new thing about "this" thing.

Humans keep on learning something using information and the emotions they perceive from their experiences.

Love is care. But What is Good care what is bad care? What you should care about or what you should not?

Parents care for their children, siblings care for each other, friends care for each other, people care for their gadgets, people care for their careers, people care for their appearance, people care for their health, people care for their money, etc.

When you care you love, when you don't care you don't love. The five basic rules of your mental peace are "How?, What?, Which?, When?, Why?. Ask Yourself

Money is the common thing involved in everything so money is the thing that acts like a charge in a smartphone without which the smartphone will not work. Talk about money, Think about money, work for money, and Share information for money because money is everywhere.

Expectation from something is good when it comes to money or knowledge. You can evaluate the value of something using money but you cannot evaluate the value of knowledge using money. As different people can teach you the English alphabet but the fee of teachers will vary according to time and place, there is no common principle and except knowledge, most things can be evaluated using money.

What is a Relationship? When two people decide to spend time with each other

Different factors act as a bridge to make any relationship successful sometimes it is physical appearance, sometimes it is money, and sometimes both, it depends. What is a Good Physical Appearance? Let us say two people are living in different countries, the definition of good physical appearance will depend on the type of face their eyes are habituated to looking at, There is a saying "Beauty is in the eyes of the beholder".

The meaning of good looks will again vary then how to decide whether this is good physical appearance and this is not, when people talk about being beautiful some of them will consider only good looks and some of them will consider good looks along with the way someone walks, the way someone talks and sometimes also the behavior. So being beautiful is a much broader perspective where people take many things into consideration and good physical appearance depends upon the data someone has in their mind and the definition of good physical appearance according to them. Then how to decide the criteria for good physical appearance? Everybody is beautiful.

Then why do people compliment good looks? Because everybody wants to see a smiling face in front of them, to make the other person happy because maybe they care for them or they want something in return and that something can be a return compliment sometimes too. Or they just know the common words through which most people get happiness. To make the environment comfortable and happy. Spread Compliments.

III

Happiness and Sadness

Everybody wants to be happy but what is being happy? Humans expect something in return for the work done and when they do not get the expected return they feel sadness. Happiness and sadness depend on the type of hormones released in the human body. When you do "something" again and again they develop the habit of doing it and the habit creates confidence. Like when you cook noodles, when you know how to cook you are confident when you don't know how to cook you are not confident. Confidence comes from practice and practice comes from the knowledge of how to do it. Everything in this world has a cause and an effect. As you sleep in your room the bulb glows now to switch off that bulb you need to get up from the bed and switch it off it will not just switch off itself. Here the cause is you getting up from bed and switching it off and the effect is the bulb stops glowing. When the bulb does not stop glowing you feel bad because you expected the switch to work fine as you invested your energy in getting up from bed and time too.

An employee works for the whole month and expects a salary, a businessman sells something and expects money, a teacher teaches students and expects fees and good grades from their students, people purchase a gadget and expect it to work fine for some time, people purchase a book and expect good information, it is the expectations that create want in the human mind.

Everything starts from thinking about something, when you think about something that creates your attachment to that thing, which creates expectations, and when people do not get something that is expected they feel angry or sad. Like a student expects the same questions in the examination that he has read before the examination. when the questions are unexpected that creates anger or sadness as he knows that he will not get good grades. Then he expects the exams to get canceled, if exams get canceled he becomes happy because his expectations are met if not then he becomes sad. What is the solution? The answer is to just keep doing the right thing and not expect anything from anyone in return except money. Treat your hard work as a sacrifice, when you get something good that is unexpected you will become happy, and when you will get something bad that is unexpected you will not be sad.

What is Trust? Trust is also a form of expectation where you expect something from someone, when things go according to you then trust is good, when not, trust is bad. Is trusting bad? No, trusting is good. What happens when you toss a coin? You can get a head and you can get a tail but you expected heads. There was always a possibility of heads or tails. If you want to trust always be clear in your mind WHY?

IV

The Right

Humans live on a planet covered by an environment. Every morning the sun rises they wake up from their bed after a good sleep and start thinking about the day or they just start doing the things they do on a daily basis. The definition of right and wrong depends on many scenarios like the country they live in, the job they do, or the people they are surrounded with. It is the data that they have in their mind and the things they celebrate that makes them happy. But different people get happy from different things and get sad from different things. What is the right?

Humans live in a country and the country has a government, government has some laws, and laws are meant to be obeyed. So the right is the law or the constitution. But what if there is a country that does not has a constitution? What is right for the people of a country that does not has a constitution? It is humanity. Stop Fighting and Spread Smiles.

What is meant by humanity? There are two things on a planet one that changes shape and size and another that does not. Living organisms like humans, animals, or plants depend on the environment or nature. When human beings want water they need nature, when they want air they need nature, when they want a place to live they need nature, when they want fire they need nature, the most important and nonnegotiable thing without which humans cannot survive is nature. So to save humanity you must save nature. How?

Education is the way through which people get information when information travels from one human mind to another it creates an influence. When information reaches one human mind to another the other human mind starts thinking after thinking they start wanting and expecting after that they start talking and start influencing other human beings. So to make a good change the influence must be good and for good influence, the exchange of ideas must be good and for good ideas, Education must be good. The Right is Education when the Education is right.

I give priority to the words when people speak, the tone of voice and the words used helps to create an emotion. Everybody likes to hear something good, Do talk to everybody nicely. But the definition of "something good" also depends on the words they care about, the meaning of those words that they have in their minds, and the past emotions attached to those words. You cannot make everybody happy, so to be on the safe side, talk to everybody nicely. Be Neutral, Do not react too much when you get happiness because that too shall pass, and do not react too much when you get sadness because that too shall pass. Life is like a graph of the stock market sometimes it goes up, and sometimes it goes down. It depends whether you chose the "call" or the "put".

V

Hope

When people hope they expect the situation to be positive and fruitful for them. Like a cook on a food stall, when he expects all the people to like the food he cooked then he will never be happy because the good taste or the bad taste of the food will depend on the customers, different customers have different reviews. But, when the cook decides to expect the sales of each day to grow with most of the people not all but most of them to like the food he cooked with a good amount of sales from which he will get a good profit, that will make the life of the cook better then that is hope.

When you ask someone a basic question about what they want from life, the answers will vary from person to person but the one thing that is common in all the answers is they all want happiness, for happiness humans need good health and peace of mind. For good health, people need good education and good money. How much money is enough for one person will again vary from another person. The answer regarding how much depends on future planning, goals, present financial position, etc., and also on the kind of enjoyment someone expects.

What is Enjoyment? What is Boring?

The meaning of the word enjoyment also depends. when you ask someone to enjoy the activities which people enjoy will vary so how to decide whether this is enjoyment and this is not? Like some people find indoor board games boring while some people enjoy them, and some people love outdoor games while some find them boring.

Then people start suggesting to other people about the kind of happiness they get from different activities, what they call enjoyment and when the activities don't match they call it this thing is boring or that thing is boring. Basically, people want to get around an environment that matches their comfort level. People want their environment to match with their desires, when the surrounding doesn't match their desirable expectation they want to change the surrounding. That creates influence.

To make the environment good the influence must be good, and good and bad depend, then how to decide what is a good influence and what is a bad influence. You have to first decide who are the people whom you never want to see sad. Most of the time it is your family, sometimes it is your friends sometimes both. When you give priority to the persons you care about the most then automatically your brain has information about the highly prioritized people and will work accordingly.

EPILOGUE

Humans depend on Nature and Nature must be protected for the children who have been born and will born and will grow in age and need the resources. The travel of information starts from thinking and talking. Everything is connected to time. There are different emotions like Happy, Sad, Anger, etc. Conflicts happen because of anger, and anger happens when you want yourself to be right all the time. Being right gives you the emotion of winning and then you celebrate which makes you happy.

The definition of righteousness depends upon the country, time, profession, etc. If humans will think before they talk or communicate they will not hurt another human. The best way is to speak less and communicate only what is necessary. But what to talk about and what is right?

To experience anything in this world humans need five senses. The Five senses and the human brain work when you have good health, Good health needs good food and a happy mind. Be always thankful for the people who gave you these five senses and always take care of them.

There are two ways humans get food either they find the seed, and land and grow by themselves which is agriculture. Another way is to buy food.

How much money is enough will always depend, BUT
Humans need money for Eating,
Humans need money for Sleeping,
Humans need money for Talking
Humans need money for Education
Humans need money for Healthcare
Humans need money for Happiness

Natural Resources must be saved and renewable sources of energy must be given high priority.

When you have enough money for yourself, take care of others. When you don't, take care of yourself first. How much is enough? It depends.

There are many things about which humans can talk, the right thing is to talk about money because money can give you good health, a good home, a happy life, and a happy mind.

Always remember to feed your brain with the right information, because the brain stores information that creates memory, and memories and information create a personality, and the things that personality does create Life.

This is a small book, save time and earn money.

Max is still sleeping. Take Care

Bhism Narayan Yadav

Printed by Libri Plureos GmbH in Hamburg,
Germany